SELECTED POEMS OF

B

Oscar W

SELECTED POEMS OF OSCAR WILDE

Published by Yurita Press

New York City, NY

First published circa 1900

Copyright © Yurita Press, 2015

All rights reserved

ABOUT YURITA PRESS

Yurita Press is a boutique publishing company run by people who are passionate about history's greatest works. We strive to republish the best books ever written across every conceivable genre and making them easily and cheaply available to readers across the world.

PREFACE

It is thought that a selection from Oscar Wilde's early verses may be of interest to a large public at present familiar only with the always popular Ballad of Reading Gaol, also included in this volume. The poems were first collected by their author when he was twenty-sex years old, and though never, until recently, well received by the critics, have survived the test of NINE editions. Readers will be able to make for themselves the obvious and striking contrasts between these first and last phases of Oscar Wilde's literary activity. The intervening period was devoted almost entirely to dramas, prose, fiction, essays, and criticism.

ROBERT ROSS

Reform Club,

NOTE

At the end of the complete text will be found a shorter version based on the original draft of the poem. This is included for the benefit of reciters and their audiences who have found the entire poem too long for declamation. I have tried to obviate a difficulty, without officiously exercising the ungrateful prerogatives of a literary executor, by falling back on a text which represents the author's first scheme for a poem—never intended of course for recitation.

ROBERT ROSS

IN MEMORIAM

C. T. W.

Sometimes trooper of

The Royal Horse Guards

Obiit H.M. Prison

Reading, Berkshire

July 7th, 1896

THE BALLAD OF READING GAOL

I

He did not wear his scarlet coat,
And blood and wine were on his hands
The poor dead woman whom he loved,
He walked amongst the Trial Men
A cricket cap was on his head,
But I never saw a man who looked

I never saw a man who looked
Upon that little tent of blue
And at every drifting cloud that went
I walked, with other souls in pain,
And was wondering if the man had done
When a voice behind me whispered low,

Dear Christ! the very prison walls
And the sky above my head became
And, though I was a soul in pain,
I only knew what hunted thought
He looked upon the garish day
The man had killed the thing he loved,

Yet each man kills the thing he loves,
Some do it with a bitter look,
The coward does it with a kiss,
Some kill their love when they are young,
Some strangle with the hands of Lust,
The kindest use a knife, because

Some love too little, some too long,
Some do the deed with many tears,
For each man kills the thing he loves,
He does not die a death of shame
Nor have a noose about his neck,
Nor drop feet foremost through the floor

He does not sit with silent men
Who watch him when he tries to weep,
Who watch him lest himself should rob
He does not wake at dawn to see
The shivering Chaplain robed in white,
And the Governor all in shiny black,
He does not rise in piteous haste

While some coarse-mouthed Doctor gloats, and notes
Fingering a watch whose little ticks
He does not know that sickening thirst
The hangman with his gardener's gloves
And binds one with three leathern thongs,
He does not bend his head to hear
Nor, while the terror of his soul
Cross his own coffin, as he moves
He does not stare upon the air
He does not pray with lips of clay
Nor feel upon his shuddering cheek

II

Six weeks our guardsman walked the yard,
His cricket cap was on his head,
But I never saw a man who looked
I never saw a man who looked
Upon that little tent of blue
And at every wandering cloud that trailed
He did not wring his hands, as do
To try to rear the changeling Hope
He only looked upon the sun,
He did not wring his hands nor weep,
But he drank the air as though it held
With open mouth he drank the sun
And I and all the souls in pain,
Forgot if we ourselves had done
And watched with gaze of dull amaze
And strange it was to see him pass
And strange it was to see him look
And strange it was to think that he
For oak and elm have pleasant leaves
But grim to see is the gallows-tree,
And, green or dry, a man must die
The loftiest place is that seat of grace
But who would stand in hempen band
And through a murderer's collar take
It is sweet to dance to violins
To dance to flutes, to dance to lutes
But it is not sweet with nimble feet
So with curious eyes and sick surmise

And wondered if each one of us
For none can tell to what red Hell
At last the dead man walked no more
And I knew that he was standing up
And that never would I see his face
Like two doomed ships that pass in storm
But we made no sign, we said no word,
For we did not meet in the holy night,
A prison wall was round us both,
The world had thrust us from its heart,
And the iron gin that waits for Sin

III

In Debtors' Yard the stones are hard,
So it was there he took the air
And by each side a Warder walked,
Or else he sat with those who watched
Who watched him when he rose to weep,
Who watched him lest himself should rob
The Governor was strong upon
The Doctor said that Death was but
And twice a day the Chaplain called,
And twice a day he smoked his pipe,
His soul was resolute, and held
He often said that he was glad
But why he said so strange a thing
For he to whom a watcher's doom
Must set a lock upon his lips,
Or else he might be moved, and try
And what should Human Pity do
What word of grace in such a place
With slouch and swing around the ring
We did not care: we knew we were
And shaven head and feet of lead
We tore the tarry rope to shreds
We rubbed the doors, and scrubbed the floors,
And, rank by rank, we soaped the plank,
We sewed the sacks, we broke the stones,
We banged the tins, and bawled the hymns,
But in the heart of every man
So still it lay that every day

And we forgot the bitter lot
Till once, as we tramped in from work,
With yawning mouth the yellow hole
The very mud cried out for blood
And we knew that ere one dawn grew fair
Right in we went, with soul intent
The hangman, with his little bag,
And each man trembled as he crept
That night the empty corridors
And up and down the iron town
And through the bars that hide the stars
He lay as one who lies and dreams
The watchers watched him as he slept,
How one could sleep so sweet a sleep
But there is no sleep when men must weep
So we—the fool, the fraud, the knave—
And through each brain on hands of pain
Alas! it is a fearful thing
For, right within, the sword of Sin
And as molten lead were the tears we shed
The Warders with their shoes of felt
And peeped and saw, with eyes of awe,
And wondered why men knelt to pray
All through the night we knelt and prayed,
The troubled plumes of midnight were
And bitter wine upon a sponge
The grey cock crew, the red cock crew,
And crooked shapes of Terror crouched,
And each evil sprite that walks by night
They glided past, they glided fast,
They mocked the moon in a rigadoon
And with formal pace and loathsome grace
With mop and mow, we saw them go,
About, about, in ghostly rout
And the damned grotesques made arabesques,
With the pirouettes of marionettes,
But with flutes of Fear they filled the ear,
And loud they sang, and long they sang,
'Oho!' they cried, 'The world is wide,
And once, or twice, to throw the dice

But he does not win who plays with Sin
No things of air these antics were,
To men whose lives were held in gyves,
Ah! wounds of Christ! they were living things,
Around, around, they waltzed and wound;
With the mincing step of a demirep
And with subtle sneer, and fawning leer,
The morning wind began to moan,
Through its giant loom the web of gloom
And, as we prayed, we grew afraid
The moaning wind went wandering round
Till like a wheel of turning steel
O moaning wind! what had we done
At last I saw the shadowed bars,
Move right across the whitewashed wall
And I knew that somewhere in the world
At six o'clock we cleaned our cells,
But the sough and swing of a mighty wing
For the Lord of Death with icy breath
He did not pass in purple pomp,
Three yards of cord and a sliding board
So with rope of shame the Herald came
We were as men who through a fen
We did not dare to breathe a prayer,
Something was dead in each of us,
For Man's grim Justice goes its way,
It slays the weak, it slays the strong,
With iron heel it slays the strong,
We waited for the stroke of eight:
For the stroke of eight is the stroke of Fate
And Fate will use a running noose
We had no other thing to do,
So, like things of stone in a valley lone,
But each man's heart beat thick and quick,
With sudden shock the prison-clock
And from all the gaol rose up a wail
Like the sound that frightened marshes hear
And as one sees most fearful things
We saw the greasy hempen rope
And heard the prayer the hangman's snare

And all the woe that moved him so
And the wild regrets, and the bloody sweats,
For he who lives more lives than one

IV

There is no chapel on the day
The Chaplain's heart is far too sick,
Or there is that written in his eyes
So they kept us close till nigh on noon,
And the Warders with their jingling keys
And down the iron stair we tramped,
Out into God's sweet air we went,
For this man's face was white with fear,
And I never saw sad men who looked
I never saw sad men who looked
Upon that little tent of blue
And at every careless cloud that passed
But there were those amongst us all
And knew that, had each got his due,
He had but killed a thing that lived,
For he who sins a second time
And draws it from its spotted shroud,
And makes it bleed great gouts of blood,
Like ape or clown, in monstrous garb
Silently we went round and round
Silently we went round and round,
Silently we went round and round,
The Memory of dreadful things
And Horror stalked before each man,
The Warders strutted up and down,
Their uniforms were spick and span,
But we knew the work they had been at,
For where a grave had opened wide,
Only a stretch of mud and sand
And a little heap of burning lime,
For he has a pall, this wretched man,
Deep down below a prison-yard,
He lies, with fetters on each foot,
And all the while the burning lime
It eats the brittle bone by night,
It eats the flesh and bone by turns,

For three long years they will not sow
For three long years the unblessed spot
And look upon the wondering sky
They think a murderer's heart would taint
It is not true! God's kindly earth
And the red rose would but blow more red,
Out of his mouth a red, red rose!
For who can say by what strange way,
Since the barren staff the pilgrim bore
But neither milk-white rose nor red
The shard, the pebble, and the flint,
For flowers have been known to heal
So never will wine-red rose or white,
On that stretch of mud and sand that lies
To tell the men who tramp the yard
Yet though the hideous prison-wall
And a spirit may not walk by night
And a spirit may but weep that lies
He is at peace—this wretched man—
There is no thing to make him mad,
For the lampless Earth in which he lies
They hanged him as a beast is hanged:
A requiem that might have brought
But hurriedly they took him out,
They stripped him of his canvas clothes,
They mocked the swollen purple throat,
And with laughter loud they heaped the shroud
The Chaplain would not kneel to pray
Nor mark it with that blessed Cross
Because the man was one of those
Yet all is well; he has but passed
And alien tears will fill for him
For his mourners will be outcast men,
V
I know not whether Laws be right,
All that we know who lie in gaol
And that each day is like a year,
But this I know, that every Law
Since first Man took his brother's life,
But straws the wheat and saves the chaff

This too I know—and wise it were
That every prison that men build
And bound with bars lest Christ should see
With bars they blur the gracious moon,
And they do well to hide their Hell,
That Son of God nor son of Man
The vilest deeds like poison weeds,
It is only what is good in Man
Pale Anguish keeps the heavy gate,
For they starve the little frightened child
And they scourge the weak, and flog the fool,
And some grow mad, and all grow bad,
Each narrow cell in which we dwell
And the fetid breath of living Death
And all, but Lust, is turned to dust
The brackish water that we drink
And the bitter bread they weigh in scales
And Sleep will not lie down, but walks
But though lean Hunger and green Thirst
We have little care of prison fare,
Is that every stone one lifts by day
With midnight always in one's heart,
We turn the crank, or tear the rope,
And the silence is more awful far
And never a human voice comes near
And the eye that watches through the door
And by all forgot, we rot and rot,
And thus we rust Life's iron chain
And some men curse, and some men weep,
But God's eternal Laws are kind
And every human heart that breaks,
Is as that broken box that gave
And filled the unclean leper's house
Ah! happy they whose hearts can break
How else may man make straight his plan
How else but through a broken heart
And he of the swollen purple throat,
Waits for the holy hands that took
And a broken and a contrite heart
The man in red who reads the Law

Three little weeks in which to heal
And cleanse from every blot of blood
And with tears of blood he cleansed the hand,
For only blood can wipe out blood,
And the crimson stain that was of Cain
VI
In Reading gaol by Reading town
And in it lies a wretched man
In a burning winding-sheet he lies,
And there, till Christ call forth the dead,
No need to waste the foolish tear,
The man had killed the thing he loved,
And all men kill the thing they love,
Some do it with a bitter look,
The coward does it with a kiss,

APPENDIXTHE BALLAD OF READING GAOL

A VERSION BASED ON THE ORIGINAL DRAFT OF THE POEM
I
He did not wear his scarlet coat,
And blood and wine were on his hands
The poor dead woman whom he loved,
He walked amongst the Trial Men
A cricket cap was on his head,
But I never saw a man who looked
I never saw a man who looked
Upon that little tent of blue
And at every drifting cloud that went
I walked, with other souls in pain,
And was wondering if the man had done
When a voice behind me whispered low,
Dear Christ! the very prison walls
And the sky above my head became
And, though I was a soul in pain,
I only knew what hunted thought
He looked upon the garish day
The man had killed the thing he loved,
Yet each man kills the thing he loves,
Some do it with a bitter look,
The coward does it with a kiss,
Some kill their love when they are young,
Some strangle with the hands of Lust,
The kindest use a knife, because
Some love too little, some too long,
Some do the deed with many tears,
For each man kills the thing he loves,
He does not die a death of shame
Nor have a noose about his neck,
Nor drop feet foremost through the floor
He does not wake at dawn to see
The shivering Chaplain robed in white,
And the Governor all in shiny black,
He does not rise in piteous haste
While some coarse-mouthed Doctor gloats, and notes
Fingering a watch whose little ticks

He does not know that sickening thirst
The hangman with his gardener's gloves
And binds one with three leathern thongs,
He does not bend his head to hear
Nor, while the terror of his soul
Cross his own coffin, as he moves
He does not stare upon the air
He does not pray with lips of clay
Nor feel upon his shuddering cheek

II

Six weeks our guardsman walked the yard,
His cricket cap was on his head,
But I never saw a man who looked
He did not wring his hands nor weep,
But he drank the air as though it held
With open mouth he drank the sun
And I and all the souls in pain,
Forgot if we ourselves had done
And watched with gaze of dull amaze
So with curious eyes and sick surmise
And wondered if each one of us
For none can tell to what red Hell
At last the dead man walked no more
And I knew that he was standing up
And that never would I see his face
Like two doomed ships that pass in storm
But we made no sign, we said no word,
For we did not meet in the holy night,
A prison wall was round us both,
The world had thrust us from its heart,
And the iron gin that waits for Sin

III

In Debtors' Yard the stones are hard,
So it was there he took the air
And by each side a Warder walked,
Or else he sat with those who watched
Who watched him when he rose to weep,
Who watched him lest himself should rob
And twice a day he smoked his pipe,
His soul was resolute, and held

He often said that he was glad
But why he said so strange a thing
For he to whom a watcher's doom
Must set a lock upon his lips,
With slouch and swing around the ring
We did not care: we knew we were
And shaven head and feet of lead
We tore the tarry rope to shreds
We rubbed the doors, and scrubbed the floors,
And, rank by rank, we soaped the plank,
We sewed the sacks, we broke the stones,
We banged the tins, and bawled the hymns,
But in the heart of every man
So still it lay that every day
And we forgot the bitter lot
Till once, as we tramped in from work,
Right in we went, with soul intent
The hangman, with his little bag,
And each man trembled as he crept
That night the empty corridors
And up and down the iron town
And through the bars that hide the stars
But there is no sleep when men must weep
So we—the fool, the fraud, the knave—
And through each brain on hands of pain
Alas! it is a fearful thing
For, right within, the sword of Sin
And as molten lead were the tears we shed
The Warders with their shoes of felt
And peeped and saw, with eyes of awe,
And wondered why men knelt to pray
The morning wind began to moan,
Through its giant loom the web of gloom
And, as we prayed, we grew afraid
At last I saw the shadowed bars,
Move right across the whitewashed wall
And I knew that somewhere in the world
At six o'clock we cleaned our cells,
But the sough and swing of a mighty wing
For the Lord of Death with icy breath

He did not pass in purple pomp,
Three yards of cord and a sliding board
So with rope of shame the Herald came
We waited for the stroke of eight:
For the stroke of eight is the stroke of Fate
And Fate will use a running noose
We had no other thing to do,
So, like things of stone in a valley lone,
But each man's heart beat thick and quick,
With sudden shock the prison-clock
And from all the gaol rose up a wail
Like the sound that frightened marshes hear
And as one sees most fearful things
We saw the greasy hempen rope
And heard the prayer the hangman's snare
And all the woe that moved him so
And the wild regrets, and the bloody sweats,
For he who lives more lives than one
IV
There is no chapel on the day
The Chaplain's heart is far too sick,
Or there is that written in his eyes
So they kept us close till nigh on noon,
And the Warders with their jingling keys
And down the iron stair we tramped,
Out into God's sweet air we went,
For this man's face was white with fear,
And I never saw sad men who looked
I never saw sad men who looked
Upon that little tent of blue
And at every careless cloud that passed
But there were those amongst us all
And knew that, had each got his due,
He had but killed a thing that lived,
For he who sins a second time
And draws it from its spotted shroud,
And makes it bleed great gouts of blood,
Like ape or clown, in monstrous garb
Silently we went round and round
Silently we went round and round,

Silently we went round and round,
The Memory of dreadful things
And Horror stalked before each man,
The Warders strutted up and down,
Their uniforms were spick and span,
But we knew the work they had been at,
For where a grave had opened wide,
Only a stretch of mud and sand
And a little heap of burning lime,
For he has a pall, this wretched man,
Deep down below a prison-yard,
He lies, with fetters on each foot,
For three long years they will not sow
For three long years the unblessed spot
And look upon the wondering sky
They think a murderer's heart would taint
It is not true! God's kindly earth
And the red rose would but blow more red,
Out of his mouth a red, red rose!
For who can say by what strange way,
Since the barren staff the pilgrim bore
But neither milk-white rose nor red
The shard, the pebble, and the flint,
For flowers have been known to heal
So never will wine-red rose or white,
On that stretch of mud and sand that lies
To tell the men who tramp the yard
He is at peace—this wretched man—
There is no thing to make him mad,
For the lampless Earth in which he lies
The Chaplain would not kneel to pray
Nor mark it with that blessed Cross
Because the man was one of those
Yet all is well; he has but passed
And alien tears will fill for him
For his mourners will be outcast men,

POEMSAVE IMPERATRIX

Set in this stormy Northern sea,
England! what shall men say of thee,
The earth, a brittle globe of glass,
And through its heart of crystal pass,

The spears of crimson-suited war,
And all the deadly fires which are
The yellow leopards, strained and lean,
With gaping blackened jaws are seen

The strong sea-lion of England's wars
To battle with the storm that mars
The brazen-throated clarion blows
And the high steeps of Indian snows

And many an Afghan chief, who lies
Clutches his sword in fierce surmise
The fleet-foot Marri scout, who comes
The measured roll of English drums

For southern wind and east wind meet
England with bare and bloody feet
O lonely Himalayan height,
Where saw'st thou last in clanging flight

The almond-groves of Samarcand,
And Oxus, by whose yellow sand
And on from thence to Ispahan,
Whence the long dusty caravan

And that dread city of Cabool
Whose marble tanks are ever full
Where through the narrow straight Bazaar
Is led, a present from the Czar

Here have our wild war-eagles flown,
But the sad dove, that sits alone
In vain the laughing girl will lean
Down in some treacherous black ravine,

And many a moon and sun will see
To climb upon their father's knee;
Pale women who have lost their lord
Some tarnished epaulette—some sword—

For not in quiet English fields
Where we might deck their broken shields

For some are by the Delhi walls,
And many where the Ganges falls
And some in Russian waters lie,
The portals to the East, or by
O wandering graves! O restless sleep!
O still ravine! O stormy deep!
And thou whose wounds are never healed,
O Cromwell's England! must thou yield
Go! crown with thorns thy gold-crowned head,
Wind and wild wave have got thy dead,
Wave and wild wind and foreign shore
Lips that thy lips shall kiss no more,
What profit now that we have bound
If hidden in our heart is found
What profit that our galleys ride,
Ruin and wreck are at our side,
Where are the brave, the strong, the fleet?
Wild grasses are their burial-sheet,
O loved ones lying far away,
O wasted dust! O senseless clay!
Peace, peace! we wrong the noble dead
Though childless, and with thorn-crowned head,
Yet when this fiery web is spun,
The young Republic like a sun

TO MY WIFE WITH A COPY OF MY POEMS

I can write no stately proem
From a poet to a poem
For if of these fallen petals
Love will waft it till it settles
And when wind and winter harden
It will whisper of the garden,

MAGDALEN WALKS

[After gaining the Berkeley Gold Medal for Greek at Trinity College, Dublin, in 1874, Oscar Wilde proceeded to Oxford, where he obtained a demyship at Magdalen College. He is the only real poet on the books of that institution.]

The little white clouds are racing over the sky,
Sways and swings as the thrush goes hurrying by.
A delicate odour is borne on the wings of the morning breeze,
Hopping from branch to branch on the rocking trees.
And all the woods are alive with the murmur and sound of Spring,
Girdled round with the belt of an amethyst ring.
And the plane to the pine-tree is whispering some tale of love
Of the burnished rainbow throat and the silver breast of a dove.
See! the lark starts up from his bed in the meadow there,
The kingfisher flies like an arrow, and wounds the air.

THEOCRITUS A VILLANELLE

O singer of Persephone!
Dost thou remember Sicily?
Still through the ivy flits the bee
O Singer of Persephone!
Simætha calls on Hecate
Dost thou remember Sicily?
Still by the light and laughing sea
O Singer of Persephone!
And still in boyish rivalry
Dost thou remember Sicily?
Slim Lacon keeps a goat for thee,
O Singer of Persephone!
Dost thou remember Sicily?

GREECE

The sea was sapphire coloured, and the sky
Burned like a heated opal through the air;
For the blue lands that to the eastward lie.
From the steep prow I marked with quickening eye
And all the flower-strewn hills of Arcady.
The flapping of the sail against the mast,
The only sounds:—when 'gan the West to burn,
Katakolo.

PORTIA TO ELLEN TERRY

(Written at the Lyceum Theatre)
I marvel not Bassanio was so bold
Or that Morocco's fiery heart grew cold:
For in that gorgeous dress of beaten gold
Was half so fair as thou whom I behold.
Yet fairer when with wisdom as your shield
And would not let the laws of Venice yield
I think I will not quarrel with the Bond.

FABIEN DEI FRANCHI TO MY FRIEND HENRY IRVING

The silent room, the heavy creeping shade,
The ghost's white fingers on thy shoulders laid,
And then the lonely duel in the glade,
These things are well enough,—but thou wert made
For thee should lure his love, and desperate fear
Pluck Richard's recreant dagger from its sheath—

PHÈDRE TO SARAH BERNHARDT

How vain and dull this common world must seem
At Florence with Mirandola, or walked
Through the cool olives of the Academe:
Thou should'st have gathered reeds from a green stream
Where grave Odysseus wakened from his dream.
Ah! surely once some urn of Attic clay
For thou wert weary of the sunless day,

SONNET

ON HEARING THE DIES IRÆ SUNG IN THE SISTINE CHAPEL

Nay, Lord, not thus! white lilies in the spring,
Sad olive-groves, or silver-breasted dove,
Than terrors of red flame and thundering.
The hillside vines dear memories of Thee bring:
I think it is of Thee the sparrows sing.
Come rather on some autumn afternoon,
And the fields echo to the gleaner's song,
Come when the splendid fulness of the moon

AVE MARIA GRATIA PLENA

Was this His coming! I had hoped to see
Broke open bars and fell on Danae:
Or a dread vision as when Semele
Caught her brown limbs and slew her utterly:
With such glad dreams I sought this holy place,
Some kneeling girl with passionless pale face,
Florence.

LIBERTATIS SACRA FAMES

Albeit nurtured in democracy,
Is crowned above his fellows, yet I see,
Spite of this modern fret for Liberty,
Our freedom with the kiss of anarchy.
Wherefore I love them not whose hands profane
Arts, Culture, Reverence, Honour, all things fade,

ROSES AND RUE

(To L. L.)
Could we dig up this long-buried treasure,
We never could learn love's song,
Could the passionate past that is fled
Could we live it all over again,
I remember we used to meet
And you warbled each pretty word
And your voice had a quaver in it,
And shook, as the blackbird's throat
And your eyes, they were green and grey
But lit into amethyst
And your mouth, it would never smile
Then it rippled all over with laughter
You were always afraid of a shower,
I remember you started and ran
I remember I never could catch you,
You had wonderful, luminous, fleet,
I remember your hair—did I tie it?
Like a tangled sunbeam of gold:
I remember so well the room,
That beat at the dripping pane
And the colour of your gown,
And two yellow satin bows
And the handkerchief of French lace
Had a small tear left a stain?
On your hand as it waved adieu
In your voice as it said good-bye
'You have only wasted your life.'
When I rushed through the garden gate
Could we live it over again,
Could the passionate past that is fled
Well, if my heart must break,
It will break in music, I know,
But strange that I was not told
In a tiny ivory cell

FROM 'THE GARDEN OF EROS'

[In this poem the author laments the growth of materialism in the nineteenth century. He hails Keats and Shelley and some of the poets and artists who were his contemporaries, although his seniors, as the torch-bearers of the intellectual life. Among these are Swinburne, William Morris, Rossetti, and Brune-Jones.]

Nay, when Keats died the Muses still had left
But ah! too soon of it we were bereft
Panthea claimed her singer as her own,
And slew the mouth that praised her; since which time we walk alone,
Save for that fiery heart, that morning star
Saw from our tottering throne and waste of war
Rise mightily like Hesperus and bring
The great Republic! him at least thy love hath taught to sing,
And he hath been with thee at Thessaly,
In passionless and fierce virginity
Hath pierced the cavern of the hollow hill,
And Venus laughs to know one knee will bow before her still.
And he hath kissed the lips of Proserpine,
That wounded forehead dashed with blood and wine
Have found their last, most ardent worshipper,
And the new Sign grows grey and dim before its conqueror.
Spirit of Beauty! tarry with us still,
The star that shook above the Eastern hill
From all the gathering gloom and fretful fight—
O tarry with us still! for through the long and common night,
Morris, our sweet and simple Chaucer's child,
With soft and sylvan pipe has oft beguiled
And from the far and flowerless fields of ice
Has brought fair flowers to make an earthly paradise.
We know them all, Gudrun the strong men's bride,
How giant Grettir fought and Sigurd died,
When lonely Brynhild wrestled with the powers
That war against all passion, ah! how oft through summer hours,
Long listless summer hours when the noon
Forgets to journey westward, till the moon
From a thin sickle to a silver shield
And chides its loitering car—how oft, in some cool grassy field
Far from the cricket-ground and noisy eight,
Almost before the blackbird finds a mate

Of many murmuring bees flits through the leaves,
Have I lain poring on the dreamy tales his fancy weaves,
And through their unreal woes and mimic pain
And in their simple mirth grew glad again;
The strength and splendour of the storm was mine
Without the storm's red ruin, for the singer is divine;
The little laugh of water falling down
Close hoarded in the tiny waxen town
Half-withered reeds that waved in Arcady
Touched by his lips break forth again to fresher harmony.
Spirit of Beauty, tarry yet awhile!
With iron roads profane our lovely isle,
Ay! though the crowded factories beget
The blindworm Ignorance that slays the soul, O tarry yet!
For One at least there is,—He bears his name
Whose double laurels burn with deathless flame
Who saw old Merlin lured in Vivien's snare,
And the white feet of angels coming down the golden stair,
Loves thee so well, that all the World for him
And Sorrow take a purple diadem,
Gild its own thorns, and Pain, like Adon, be
Even in anguish beautiful;—such is the empery
Which Painters hold, and such the heritage
Being a better mirror of his age
Than those who can but copy common things,
And leave the Soul unpainted with its mighty questionings.
But they are few, and all romance has flown,
And lecture on his arrows—how, alone,
How from each tree its weeping nymph has fled,
And that no more 'mid English reeds a Naiad shows her head.

THE HARLOT'S HOUSE

We caught the tread of dancing feet,
We loitered down the moonlit street,
And stopped beneath the harlot's house.
Inside, above the din and fray,
We heard the loud musicians play
The 'Treues Liebes Herz' of Strauss.
Like strange mechanical grotesques,
Making fantastic arabesques,
The shadows raced across the blind.
We watched the ghostly dancers spin
To sound of horn and violin,
Like black leaves wheeling in the wind.
Like wire-pulled automatons,
Slim silhouetted skeletons
Went sidling through the slow quadrille,
Then took each other by the hand,
And danced a stately saraband;
Their laughter echoed thin and shrill.
Sometimes a clockwork puppet pressed
A phantom lover to her breast,
Sometimes they seemed to try to sing.
Sometimes a horrible marionette
Came out, and smoked its cigarette
Upon the steps like a live thing.
Then, turning to my love, I said,
'The dead are dancing with the dead,
The dust is whirling with the dust.'
But she—she heard the violin,
And left my side, and entered in:
Love passed into the house of lust.
Then suddenly the tune went false,
The dancers wearied of the waltz,
The shadows ceased to wheel and whirl.
And down the long and silent street,
The dawn, with silver-sandalled feet,
Crept like a frightened girl.

FROM 'THE BURDEN OF ITYS'

This English Thames is holier far than Rome,
Breaking across the woodland, with the foam
To fleck their blue waves,—God is likelier there
Than hidden in that crystal-hearted star the pale monks bear!
Those violet-gleaming butterflies that take
Are monsignores, and where the rushes shake
His eyes half shut,—he is some mitred old
Bishop in partibus! look at those gaudy scales all green and gold.
The wind the restless prisoner of the trees
The mighty master's hands were on the keys
When early on some sapphire Easter morn
In a high litter red as blood or sin the Pope is borne
From his dark House out to the Balcony
Whose very fountains seem for ecstasy
And stretching out weak hands to East and West
In vain sends peace to peaceless lands, to restless nations rest.
Is not yon lingering orange after-glow
Rome's lordliest pageants! strange, a year ago
Who bare the Host across the Esquiline,
And now—those common poppies in the wheat seem twice as fine.
The blue-green beanfields yonder, tremulous
Through this cool evening than the odorous
When the grey priest unlocks the curtained shrine,
And makes God's body from the common fruit of corn and vine.
Poor Fra Giovanni bawling at the Mass
Sings overhead, and through the long cool grass
On starlit hills of flower-starred Arcady,
Once where the white and crescent sand of Salamis meets sea.
Sweet is the swallow twittering on the eaves
And stock-doves murmur, and the milkmaid leaves
To see the heavy-lowing cattle wait
Stretching their huge and dripping mouths across the farmyard gate.
And sweet the hops upon the Kentish leas,
And sweet the fretful swarms of grumbling bees
And sweet the heifer breathing in the stall,
And the green bursting figs that hang upon the red-brick wall,
And sweet to hear the cuckoo mock the spring
And sweet to hear the shepherd Daphnis sing

Of warm Arcadia where the corn is gold
And the slight lithe-limbed reapers dance about the wattled fold.
* * * * *

It was a dream, the glade is tenantless,
The Thames creeps on in sluggish leadenness,
Fled is young Bacchus with his revelry,
Yet still from Nuneham wood there comes that thrilling melody
So sad, that one might think a human heart
Which music sometimes has, being the Art
Poor mourning Philomel, what dost thou fear?
Thy sister doth not haunt these fields, Pandion is not here,
Here is no cruel Lord with murderous blade,
But mossy dells for roving comrades made,
With half-shut book, and many a winding walk
Where rustic lovers stray at eve in happy simple talk.
The harmless rabbit gambols with its young
A troop of laughing boys in jostling throng
The gossamer, with ravelled silver threads,
Works at its little loom, and from the dusky red-eaved sheds
Of the lone Farm a flickering light shines out
Back to their wattled sheep-cotes, a faint shout
And starts the moor-hen from the sedgy rill,
And the dim lengthening shadows flit like swallows up the hill.
The heron passes homeward to the mere,
Gold world by world the silent stars appear,
A white moon drifts across the shimmering sky,
Mute arbitress of all thy sad, thy rapturous threnody.
She does not heed thee, wherefore should she heed,
'Tis I, 'tis I, whose soul is as the reed
So pipes another's bidding, it is I,
Drifting with every wind on the wide sea of misery.
Ah! the brown bird has ceased: one exquisite trill
Dying in music, else the air is still,
Wander and wheel above the pines, or tell
Each tiny dew-drop dripping from the bluebell's brimming cell.
And far away across the lengthening wold,
Magdalen's tall tower tipped with tremulous gold
And warns me to return; I must not wait,
Hark! 't is the curfew booming from the bell at Christ Church gate.

FLOWER OF LOVE

Sweet, I blame you not, for mine the fault
was, had I not been made of common clay
I had climbed the higher heights unclimbed
yet, seen the fuller air, the larger day.
From the wildness of my wasted passion I had
struck a better, clearer song,
Lit some lighter light of freer freedom, battled
with some Hydra-headed wrong.
Had my lips been smitten into music by the
kisses that but made them bleed,
You had walked with Bice and the angels on
that verdant and enamelled mead.
I had trod the road which Dante treading saw
the suns of seven circles shine,
Ay! perchance had seen the heavens opening,
as they opened to the Florentine.
And the mighty nations would have crowned
me, who am crownless now and without name,
And some orient dawn had found me kneeling
on the threshold of the House of Fame.
I had sat within that marble circle where the
oldest bard is as the young,
And the pipe is ever dropping honey, and the
lyre's strings are ever strung.
Keats had lifted up his hymeneal curls from out
the poppy-seeded wine,
With ambrosial mouth had kissed my forehead,
clasped the hand of noble love in mine.
And at springtide, when the apple-blossoms
brush the burnished bosom of the dove,
Two young lovers lying in an orchard would
have read the story of our love;
Would have read the legend of my passion,
known the bitter secret of my heart,
Kissed as we have kissed, but never parted as
we two are fated now to part.
For the crimson flower of our life is eaten by
the cankerworm of truth,

And no hand can gather up the fallen withered
petals of the rose of youth.
Yet I am not sorry that I loved you—ah!
what else had I a boy to do,—
For the hungry teeth of time devour, and the
silent-footed years pursue.
Rudderless, we drift athwart a tempest, and
when once the storm of youth is past,
Without lyre, without lute or chorus, Death
the silent pilot comes at last.
And within the grave there is no pleasure,
for the blindworm battens on the root,
And Desire shudders into ashes, and the tree
of Passion bears no fruit.
Ah! what else had I to do but love you?
God's own mother was less dear to me,
And less dear the Cytheræan rising like an
argent lily from the sea.
I have made my choice, have lived my
poems, and, though youth is gone in wasted days,
I have found the lover's crown of myrtle better
than the poet's crown of bays.

FOOTNOTES

Shelley.
Swinburne.
Rossetti.
Burne-Jones.

19769163R00024

Printed in Great Britain
by Amazon